THE WOODCUTTER'S DUCK

KRYSTYNA TURSKA

The Macmillan Company, New York, New York

First published in Great Britain by Hamish Hamilton Children's Books Ltd. 1972

Once long ago in the mountains of Poland there lived
a young man, a woodcutter, whose name was
Bartek. He was very poor, and lived alone in a little hut
with a duck as his only companion. He had no wife and
no friends. All the girls and boys of the village would
laugh and run away when Bartek appeared in the
square with the duck at his heels.

The duck went everywhere with him and he loved her
dearly. He spent hours of his time searching for the food
she liked best, and carried water weeds and moss from
the ponds in the forest back to the hut for her in a large
sieve.

One day Bartek set off up a steep path through the trees that led to one of these ponds. The sun blazed down, and Bartek strode along whistling. As he passed a patch of bushes he heard a faint echo of the tune he was whistling, and stopped to listen.

A voice came gently to his ears:

"Help me, Bartek, please help me!"

He looked up and down the road but there was nobody to be seen.

The whisper came again, fainter than before. "Help me, Bartek! Look under the wild rose."

Bartek pushed branches and creepers apart and saw, caught among the thorny stems of the dog-rose bush, a large

green frog. Its skin was withered and
dry, and it was panting for breath.

"Help me, Bartek, please!" it gasped.
"Carry me to the pond in your sieve.
I need water badly—I've been trapped
in the thorns for so long that if I am
left like this much longer I shall die.
I am the King of the Frogs, and I shall
repay you richly one day for your
kindness."

"Of course I shall help you," said
Bartek, "and I don't expect anything
in return."

He put a layer of leaves and moss in
the bottom of the sieve, pulled the stems
of the rose bush aside and freed the Frog
King from their thorns.

As soon as they reached the pond the frog hopped into the water. At once his skin began to gleam and his breathing became easier. His voice grew stronger too.

"Come close," he said, "and listen to me. I am going to give you a magic power which you will find valuable sooner than you think. If you whistle this tune, a great storm will start to blow, with thunder and lightning so violent that it can split mountains, and with cloudbursts of rain that can flood the tallest buildings. To stop the storm, you whistle again."

Bartek thanked the Frog King and started off on his journey home. Before he got there he suddenly heard an unexpected noise—the sound of horses' hoofs and tramping feet.

Marching and riding down the winding
road was an army of thousands of men.

At the head of the procession rode the
commander, the Great Hetman.

Bartek stood back humbly to let the ranks of marching men pass by, but the Great Hetman noticed him.

"Hey you!" he shouted. "What is your name?"

"They call me Bartek," he answered, bowing low.

"Show me to the best house there is, and I shall spend the night there," said the Great Hetman.

"There are no great houses here, Sir. There is only my humble hut. You are welcome to rest in it and share my bread and milk," said Bartek, and led the way to his home.

The Great Hetman dismounted, helped by his attendants.
By ill luck, just at that moment the duck walked out
of the hut to greet her master.

    "A duck, eh!" said the Great Hetman. "I'm very
hungry. Make a fire and roast this duck for my supper."

At these dreadful words Bartek fell on his knees in front of the Great Hetman, begging him to spare his beloved friend.

"No," said the Great Hetman. "My order must be obeyed."

Bartek looked at the proud angry face with its big moustache, and his heart stood still. Then he remembered the new magical power that the Frog King had given him. Now, if ever, was the time to test it.

He whistled loudly in the way the frog had taught him.

At once a terrible peal of thunder crashed out and a
howling wind began to blow. The soldiers were plucked
out of their saddles and sent swirling through the air.
The Great Hetman too was snatched up, still clutching
his staff, and flung up to the roof of the hut. There he
crouched, holding on to the chimney.

"To me, all officers and men!" he yelled as the wind
hurtled his soldiers past him, like falling leaves in the
autumn.

Bartek looked on in amazement. The rout of the army was so complete that he began to feel sorry for the Great Hetman.

"I have the power to stop this storm at my command, just as I had the power to raise it," he shouted in the direction of the figure clinging on to the roof.

"Do you still mean to eat my duck for supper?"

"No—a piece of bread and some milk will be enough for me," cried the Great Hetman. "Help! Hurry and rescue me."

Bartek whistled again, and as suddenly as it had started, the storm stopped.

The Great Hetman was helped down from the roof of
the hut, and found his soldiers were standing to
attention, all safely back on the ground.

But as soon as he saw he was safe, the Great Hetman
broke his promise to Bartek. "Roast that duck for my
supper!" he ordered again.

This time Bartek felt more angry than frightened.
"No, Sir, you shall never eat her!" he said, and again he
whistled the tune that the Frog King had taught him.

Immediately the sky grew black.
Rain came pouring down with
such force that in a few seconds
the ground was flooded. The water
rose and rose until the whole army,
the Great Hetman included, were
up to their necks in it.

Bartek, with his duck at his feet,

looked down at the ridiculous sight. "Do you still want to eat my friend?" he asked.

"I shall never touch her—I won't let anyone lay a finger on a feather of hers," said the Great Hetman. "I promise. Just stop this rain!"

Yet again Bartek whistled, and at once the rain stopped. The floods of water went down as quickly as they had appeared, and the sun came out, drying the soldiers' soaking uniforms.

But the soldiers felt ashamed of their leader and realized that he couldn't be trusted any longer.

They turned on the Great Hetman, tore off his scarlet
cape and took his staff away from him, leaving him
standing there disgraced and alone.

Going up to Bartek, they said, "You are a greater
man than he is. Be our new commander." They placed
the cape on his shoulders and put the staff in his hand.
Then they helped him to mount the commander's horse
and cheered him loudly. "Long live Bartek!" they
shouted.

Bartek was astonished but proud and pleased to hear these words. Only one thing was missing.

"Before we leave," he said, "I must have my duck. Please bring her to me."

So the duck was brought and put on his saddle.

The army moved off, a glorious sight with its handsome
new commander Bartek at its head. And so they left the
village where Bartek had grown up, and set off in quest
of fresh triumphs for the army, and a new life for Bartek
and his duck.